# Big Cheeks
## at Squirrely Beach

Written and Illustrated by
Laura Planck
Sandcastle by Dig It!

Squirrely Beach is a fun and happy place by the ocean. This is where the ground squirrels run and play all day long.

They live here with all their friends and one squirrel loving dog named Angel.

Big Cheeks and his friends keep the beach safe for all the silly, sandy squirrels.

Squirrely

Whirrely

Boogie

Board

Contest

Today is the big Boogie Board Contest.
Everyone that boogies can enter.

There's lots of fun on the beach before the contest begins. The silly squirrels like to build sandcastles * and play hide and seek.

Angel likes to find them! They are really good at hiding from her.

Everyone has a seat to watch the Squirrely Whirrely Contest. All the good rocks are taken.

Angel, Sharkey, Skipper and Corkey
are warming up in the ocean waiting to start
the contest.

The waves are just the right size and the
water is a pretty boogie blue.

Sharkey was waiting for a big wave so he took a nap on his board. He woke up in the shallow water and said,"Yikees! Where am I?"

"Oh no!!" said Big Cheeks to Pelican Pete. "Sharky is in trouble. He's too close to the shore and can't swim back out." We have to help him!"

Big Cheeks told Romey, "Get a life preserver and rope. Give it to Pelican Pete so he can fly over to pick up Sharkey."

Pelican Pete flew as fast as he could to get there in time to save Sharkey from the shallow water.

The joy of the Lord is my strength.

The joy of the Lord is my strength.

All the fans shouted, "Hooraaay for Pelican Pete!"
Sharkey is safe and will be able to
board another day.

The contest ended. Corkey won 1st place. He was very happy and said, "Thanks dudes. I love to boogie!"

When everyone was gone, Big Cheeks
and Romey gave each other a high five and said,
"Thank you God for another safe
day at Squirrely Beach."

This is a work of fiction. All of the characters, names, incidents, organizations, and dialogue in this novel are either the products of the author's imagination or are used fictitiously.

WestBow Press books may be ordered through booksellers or by contacting:

WestBow Press
A Division of Thomas Nelson & Zondervan
1663 Liberty Drive
Bloomington, IN 47403
www.westbowpress.com
1 (866) 928-1240

Because of the dynamic nature of the Internet, any web addresses or links contained in this book may have changed since publication and may no longer be valid. The views expressed in this work are solely those of the author and do not necessarily reflect the views of the publisher, and the publisher hereby disclaims any responsibility for them.

Any people depicted in stock imagery provided by Thinkstock are models, and such images are being used for illustrative purposes only.
Certain stock imagery © Thinkstock.

ISBN: 978-1-9736-0576-8 (sc)
ISBN: 978-1-9736-0575-1 (e)

Library of Congress Control Number: 2017918492

Print information available on the last page.

WestBow Press rev. date: 12/28/2017

WESTBOW
P R E S S®
A DIVISION OF THOMAS NELSON
& ZONDERVAN